Tappity-Tap! What Was That?

SCHOLASTIC

For my friend, Nancy
~ CF
Per Arianna, ti amo sempre di più
~ RJ

First published in 2009 by Scholastic Children's Books
This edition first published in 2012
by Scholastic Children's Books
Euston House, 24 Eversholt Street
London NW1 1DB
a division of Scholastic Ltd
www.scholastic.co.uk
London ~ New York ~ Toronto ~ Sydney ~ Auckland
Mexico City ~ New Delhi ~ Hong Kong

ISBN: 978 1407 13168 9

Tappity-Tap! What Was That?

by Claire Freedman &
Russell Julian

Deep in the woods, Owl, Mouse and Rabbit
were having a **Very Important Meeting**.

"This is a Very Important Meeting,"
said Owl. "We need to do something about
the Monster Of The Woods."
"I'm scared!" cried Rabbit.
"No one's safe while It's around!" squeaked Mouse.

"I've heard he's very big and horribly hairy!" gulped Mouse.
"And very, very scary," trembled Rabbit.

"Don't panic!" said Owl, handing round notes
he had written out neatly for everyone.
"I'm sure we have nothing to worry about.
But just in case, I have a plan."

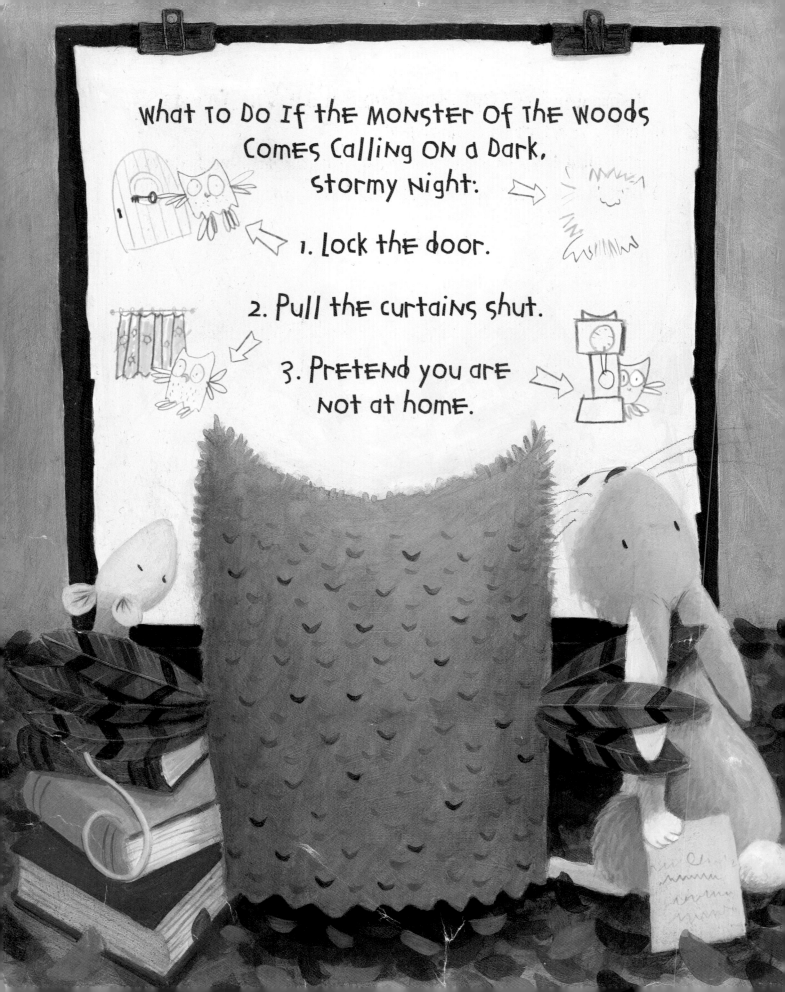

"Remember," said Owl, "the Monster Of The Woods probably won't come calling at all."

"He will if it's dark and stormy enough," shivered Rabbit.

"And if he's hungry enough!" added Mouse.

"Don't worry," said Owl. "As long as we follow my plan, we'll be safe."

That night, it was dark, and it was stormy.
Owl woke up with a start.

CRASH! BANG! CRASH!

"It's only the thunder," he thought.

HOWL! HOWL! HOWL!

"It's only the wind,"
he told himself.

Tappity-tap!

What was that?

Quick as he could, Owl locked the door,
pulled the curtains shut,
and pretended he was not at home.

"Let me in, Owl," called Rabbit. "I thought I heard the **Monster Of The Woods.** And I'm getting drenched!"

"Come in, Rabbit," said Owl. "It's only a nasty, noisy storm."

Rabbit scurried inside.

Tappity-tap!

What was that?

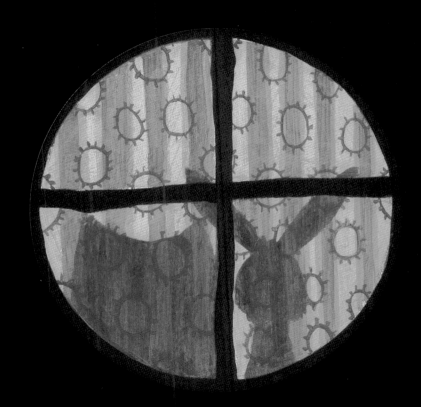

"Quick!" cried Owl. "The plan!"

So they locked the door,
pulled the curtains shut,
and pretended they were not at home.

"Come in, Mouse," said Owl.
"It's only a noisy, nasty storm."
Mouse curled up by the fire.

"Let me in, Owl," called Mouse.
"I thought I heard the
Monster Of The Woods.
And I'm freezing!"

Owl made some nice hot cocoa.
"See?" he said. "We're all safe now."

Tappity-tap-TAP!

What was that?

Rabbit dropped his mug in fright.

"Is that Mouse knocking on the front door?" he whispered.

"I'm already here, silly," Mouse squeaked.

"Is it Owl then?" Rabbit gulped.

"I'm here, too!" Owl cried.

The friends looked at each other.

"Oh no," they all whispered together. "It must be . . .

"THE MONSTER OF THE WOODS!"

"Stay calm," shouted Owl. "Remember my plan!"

So they locked the door,
pulled the curtains shut,
and pretended they were not at home.

THUMP! THUMP! THUMP!

The banging got
louder and louder...

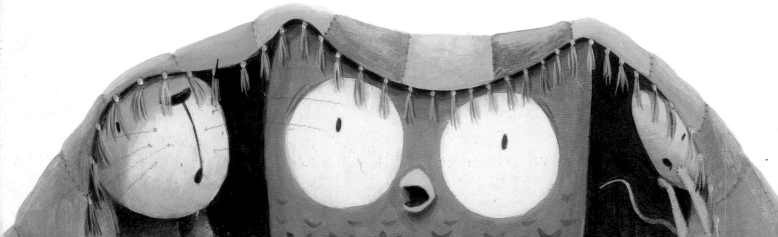

"Sniffle... snuffle... **squeak!**"

"That noise doesn't sound like a monster,"
frowned Rabbit, forgetting to pretend
they were not at home.

"It sounds like crying," said Mouse,
nervously opening the curtains.
"Whoever it is sounds frightened,"
agreed Owl. "Maybe they need help."
He peeped through the peephole...

Slowly, Owl unlocked the door.
A tiny bedraggled furry thing stood on the doorstep.

"Who are YOU?" everyone gasped.

"I'm the Monster of The Woods!"

"You?" said Mouse. "You're not very big!"
"I'm bigger than you," It said.
"You're not horribly hairy, either!" added Rabbit.
"I flatten in the rain," It replied.
"And you're not at all scary," said Owl.

"It's true," the Monster sighed.
"I don't know why everyone is so
frightened of me!"

CRASH! BANG! CRASH!

The Monster leapt into Owl's arms.
"I hate thunder!" he whimpered.
"There, there," Owl patted him kindly.
"We're all safe now."

It was the next Very Important Meeting.
Owl handed round notes he had written
out neatly for everyone.
"Before we begin," Owl beamed,
"let's welcome. . .

"the Monster Of The Woods!"
The Monster giggled,
"But my friends call me Snuggles!"
And everyone agreed,
Snuggles was the perfect name!

WHAT TO DO IF
YOU aRE STUCK UP
a tall tREE :

1. MaKE a COMFY SEat
OUT OF LEaVES.

2. WaVE a LOt.

3. SHOUt FOR HELP.

P.S. NExt WEEK BRING
PaPER aND STRING.
WE SHaLL BE
MaKING
OUR OWN
PaRaCHUtES.

The End

STAFFORDSHIRE LIBRARY AND INFORMATION SERVICES
Please return or renew by the last date shown

If not required by other readers, this item may be renewed in person, by post or telephone, online or by email.
To renew, either the book or ticket are required

24 HOUR RENEWAL LINE 0845 33 00 740